# FRED

## Wizard in Training

# SIMON PHILIP

## Illustrated by SHEENA DEMPSEY

SIMON & SCHUSTER

# Chapter One

This is a story about Fred.

Now, Fred looked like any other ordinary boy. He had two eyes, a nose and a mouth on his face, and on each side of his head was a pink, fleshy ear. As you'll know, these features are common. Rarely does a young boy have more or less than two ears, although sometimes you do hear about it. But only if you have lots of ears yourself. If you don't have any, you won't hear a thing.

Like many boys, Fred liked sausages. And chips. And ketchup. He was perfectly happy to eat them on their own, but he loved it when they all appeared on the same plate at the same time. He found toilets quite funny, as many boys do (not to mention some girls and plenty of grown-ups, too). In fact, sometimes, if the mood took him, Fred combined all of these things at once – that is to say, sausages, chips, ketchup and toilets – and had a bit of a feast while sitting on the loo. Odd, I know, but not necessarily unordinary …

Fred

Toilet

Sausage & chips

Ketchup

The thing is, sometimes even ordinary-looking boys can turn out to be not very ordinary at all. Once you know a bit more about them. Fred was one of these boys. And the reason he wasn't very ordinary is because ...

… Fred was a wizard.

Well, sort of.

It depends a bit on how you look at it.

You see, if the sort of wizard you're thinking of performs magical marvels that boggle your eyes and blow your mind, unforgettable things that make you rush to tell the nearest person … If *that's* the sort of wizard you're imagining, then Fred was definitely ***NOT*** one of them.

If, however, when you imagine a wizard they are pottering around the house, doing the boring chores that you and I do, only a little bit quicker because they can cast a spell, then, yes, Fred definitely *was* a wizard.

You might think how amazing it would be to do the washing-up without getting your hands wet, force the cat to do your homework, or be able to flick the light switch in your bedroom without ever getting out of bed. But for Fred – who could do all of these things – it was really very dull.

Chores and manipulating cats is very low-level magical stuff, you see, and – quite frankly – any wizard worth his salt doesn't really consider it magic at all. If that were all you could do (and it *was* all that Fred could do), you should be very embarrassed, they'd say.

Unfortunately for Fred, his family was full of wizards and witches worth their salt. He had three older brothers and two younger sisters, all of whom were worth a great deal of salt indeed. Salty heaps of the stuff! They were saltier than a seriously sweaty sardine swimming in Salt Lake City's lake of salt.

(By the way, if anyone asks you, 'What's the saltiest thing in the world?' you can confidently tell them it's *that* sardine.)

Fred's siblings were always showing off. Hovering in mid-air. Disappearing in a flash, then reappearing as a dog to frighten the cat. Turning chalk into cheese. Pulling hats out of rabbits (yes, you did read that correctly). Fred's eldest brother, Wallace, was so good at pulling hats out of rabbits that he held the world record for it: three hundred and forty-two hats out of the same rabbit in an hour. Luckily, he was also exceedingly charming, so Clive (the rabbit), despite being a little surprised, didn't stay upset for long. He even let Wallace keep the hats.

And Wallace wasn't the only high-

flyer in the family. Fred's three-year-old sister, Wilda, could already transform butterflies back into caterpillars, as well as count to infinity – twice. His other sister,

7,000,000,7429
7,000,000,7428
7,000,000,7427
7,000,000,7426
7,000,000,7425
7,000,000,7424
7,000,000,7423
7,000,000,7422

Willow, had somehow found a way to make lemonade from limes and was extremely popular for having invented the world's first chocolate teapot that didn't melt.

Then, of course, there were the twins, Wilbert and Wolf, who constantly reminded Fred (and everyone else for that matter) about their enormous list of accomplishments . . .

- Making fire by rubbing two ice creams together
- Pulling wheelies on unicycles
- Unscrambling scrambled eggs
- Unfrying fried eggs
- Unpoaching poached eggs
- Unlaying laid eggs (which is really quite complicated if you think about it)
- Discovering Big Foot
- Discovering the Loch Ness Monster
- Discovering the Lost Kingdom of Atlantis
- Discovering the twenty-seventh letter of the English alphabet (on the same afternoon as finding Big Foot, Nessie, Atlantis, and an old shilling down the back of the sofa)
- Wonderfully Wacky Wandwork Certificate: Advanced Level 92

- Being appointed Deputy Perma... Representatives of the Russian Federation to International Organisations in Vienna and Milton Keynes
- 2004 Royal Commendation for Raising Awareness of the Plight of Badgers Award
- Being appointed Principal Brexit Negotiators
- Becoming Honorary Members of the UN Academy of Natural Sciences
- Becoming Honorary Members of the UN Academy of Unnatural Sciences
- Swim England Rainbow Distance 10m Award (armbands and breathing apparatus permitted)

Fred didn't take *all* their claims seriously. He knew, for instance, that his brothers couldn't have discovered Einstein's Theory of Relativity before Einstein did, nor could they claim to have invented gravity or the Bermuda Triangle or cottage cheese. Even so, Fred was made to feel all the more useless and insignificant by their loud and persistent boasting.

'Oi, Fred!' they'd shout. 'Are you still doing the washing-up? I hope you don't mind but we've borrowed your wand because the magic we're doing is so advanced we need three of them, and yours never gets used properly anyway.'

His brothers and sisters were never made to waste their time or magic on household chores like Fred was. It was the only use his parents could see for Fred's limited magic, but always made him feel like the odd one out. That his parents named him Fred didn't exactly help matters, either. Why hadn't they given him a name beginning with W like the rest of his siblings? Apparently he should have been called Wilfred, but instead of correcting the mistake on his birth certificate, his parents decided to 'try something different'. It was clear as soon as Willow was born that they regretted their experiment. No wonder Fred was less magical than the rest of them: he'd been up against it from the start. And he knew he was a big disappointment to his parents. How? Because of birthday cards like the one he received this year . . .

Darling Fred,

Wishing you a very Happy Birthday!
How time flies — eight years old! Let's hope this
next year is a more magical one for you and us.
We know you try hard and that not everyone can
be as brilliant a wizard or witch as your brothers
and sisters and ourselves. There's only so much
magic to go round one family, after all. But please
try to hide your inability a little bit better.
With love (but mainly disappointment and a
sprinkling of embarrassment),

Your proud(ish) Mum & Dad

X

It was after reading this card that Fred made a decision. He had to become a better wizard. He was fed up of being the family joke. Every time his siblings made fun of him or left him out it made his heart ache. But most of all, he longed to make his parents proud. Just once. Things *had* to change. But *how*?

He didn't have a clue.

# Chapter Two

As the old saying goes: If there's anything worse than being clueless, it's being clueless in a classroom of wizards and witches half your age. (Okay, I made that saying up, but you know what I mean …)

If you thought Fred had it bad at home, he had it even worse at school. Other wizards and witches his age were already busy making lotions from potions, turning keys into monkeys and doing lots of other useful and advanced magic. Yet Fred was stuck among the youngest and tiniest of children. He felt like the twit among tots. The numpty among nippers. The airhead among amoebas.

The tots, nippers and amoebas could already cast spells to tie and untie Fred's shoelaces, even though they all wore shoes with Velcro and had never needed to tie a lace in their life. Fred couldn't even make Velcro twitch, let alone convince his laces to embrace each other. He'd only just discovered which end of his wand was which. And, hard as he tried, he was

useless at working out which wand belonged
to which witch and which witch used which
wand just by watching, which other witches
and wizards could work out in the tick of a
witch's watch. (Try saying that quickly!)

For Fred, school was an *almost* entirely miserable experience.

I say *almost* because there was one thing that stopped Fred's misery from being complete. That thing was his best friend, Marvin.

Marvin

Unlike Fred, Marvin was a brilliant and gifted wizard. So gifted that he'd been advanced into the class for the oldest and most experienced wizards at school. Sometimes when teachers were sick, the headmistress would ask Marvin to step in and take their place. This could have made Fred extremely envious, but as Marvin was so kind and modest, Fred only felt pride for his best and, well, only friend.

Of course, being in different classes meant they didn't spend as much time together as best friends normally do, but at break times and travelling to and from school they'd always be found side by side. It was the time of day they both looked forward to most.

You see, while Fred sometimes thought

he had *too many* siblings at home, Marvin hadn't got a single one. And, no matter how brilliant a wizard you are, you can't just magic a friend or a brother or a sister out of thin air (or get rid of one, for that matter). Once Marvin arrived home, it was just him and his parents. And when his parents were busy investigating top-secret and dangerous magical crimes, he had to entertain himself. With Fred, he wasn't so lonely.

Most wizards travelled around by just clicking their fingers, imagining where they wanted to go and then **POOF** they would vanish. But, as we know, Fred wasn't like most wizards, so he had to take the bus. Now, for you and me, travelling by bus is no cause for shame or embarrassment, is it?

Well, I suppose it might be if you were to do something shameful and embarrassing whilst on it, like falling asleep and dribbling down the window, or finding yourself naked when everyone else is clothed. Or, for that matter, finding yourself clothed when everyone else is naked – *that* would be awkward. Generally, though, travelling by bus is nothing to be ashamed of.

For Fred, however, it was. You see, normally, the only wizards or witches who travelled by bus were those who also couldn't poof themselves around, and included:

- Very young wizards/witches (ages four and under) who hadn't yet learned to 'click-and-go'

- Very old wizards/witches who couldn't muster the energy or magic to travel by click
- Very, very old wizards/witches who'd forgotten all about any other method of travel
- Very, very, very old wizards/witches who had lots of problems indeed
- Very, very, very, *very* old wizards/witches who had *so* many problems that it would be unkind to mention them
- Downright blooming ancient wizards/witches who were so old that they had museums or time periods named after them, despite still being alive
- Very lazy wizards/witches who preferred to travel whilst sitting on their bottoms

- Very naughty wizards/witches, who, as a means of punishment, were no longer allowed to travel by click
- Very confused wizards/witches who thought they were travelling by train
- Very, very confused wizards/witches who thought they were travelling by unicorn
- The most confused wizards/witches of all, who thought they were travelling on a train driven by a unicorn called Gary

So, as I'm sure you now understand, travelling by bus wasn't something that Fred felt proud of. Given that people on the bus were often a little bit bonkers, he also had to endure some very strange conversations. Conversations like this, for example:

'Hello.'

'Hi.'

'What time does the custard leave the abattoir?'

'Excuse me?'

'*I said*, How long is the bishop's dishwasher?'

'Pardon?'

'Which of these pheasants do you prefer? The penguin or the toilet brush?'

'Sorry, I have no idea what you're talking about.'

'That's okay. I like sawdust, too. Do you eat tiddlywinks?'

'What?'

'Got to go – need a walrus. Just remember

– whatever you do, don't trust the ka

And that was a conversation with the driver! I couldn't possibly describe Fred's talks with the passengers. Your mind would be ruined for ever.

Anyway, though Marvin could have easily **POOFED** himself straight home, he always walked with Fred to the bus stop first. He never actually got on the bus. Fred had always wondered why that was.

'Sorry, mate, I just really hate buses,' Marvin told him when he asked.

'Really? Why's that?'

'Well, for a start,' he said, 'they smell, don't they?'

'Do they? Of what?'

'Just … funny, you know. Weird. Odd. Of

things buses shouldn't.'

'Oh,' Fred said, surprised. 'I've never really noticed, to be honest.'

'Trust me, they do,' Marvin explained. 'Plus I never have the right money, and I always manage to pick a seat with chewing gum on which gets stuck to my bottom. And the passengers are always, well … strange.'

'Fair enough,' Fred said. 'You're certainly right about the passengers.' He could tell Marvin *really* didn't like buses, and, anyway, he was grateful for his friend's company for even part of his journey to and from school each day. They walked and talked, hearing each other's stories, hopes and worries. Marvin knew that Fred felt lonely sometimes too, even at home surrounded by his enormous family. After all, you don't always have to be alone to feel lonely.

It was just after he had said goodbye to Marvin at the bus stop one afternoon that Fred noticed it.

He raised his glance from the pavement to look more closely. There, on a huge poster at the bus stop, staring out at him, were two dazzling turquoise eyes. They were wise, knowing eyes that had seen majestic magic Fred could barely imagine. Above them rested the purple brim of an old pointy hat and below them a magnificent white beard flowed from cheeks like a candyfloss waterfall.

Fred's heart beat faster as he read the poster.

A WHITEBEARD PRODUCTIONS PROMOTION

Wizards and witches, daring and bold,
Stop and take note of this chance to behold!
Surrender your doubts, banish your fears,
Enter the best competition in years!

Aware of the legend, you worship his name:
Meet Merlin in person, win glory and fame!
He'll teach you some tricks, you'll bolster your magic
Whether or not it is super or tragic.

To cap it all off, he will treat you to lunch!
(Or, if you would rather, to dinner or brunch.)
This prize of a lifetime awaits for the wizard
Who captures the tail of the fearsome lizard.

But, Entrants, beware of the task up ahead:
The peril and danger fills heroes with dread.
The monster is evil, there's fire in its breath.
A fool who ignores this will meet with their death.

So summon your courage, your nerve and your skill,
Prepare for the ultimate test of your will,
And prove to the world what you're made of inside,
And fill magic hearts up with pleasure and pride.

Fred stood transfixed. He read the announcement over and over again. It was as if it was calling out to him: *fill magic hearts up with pleasure and pride.* Wasn't that exactly what he wanted to do? And he'd always dreamed of meeting Merlin – *THE* Merlin! Merlin, the greatest wizard of all time, inventor of countless incredible spells, doer of unspeakably dangerous and heroic deeds, winner of *Witches Weekly*'s Most Beautiful Beard Award for the last three hundred and seventy-six years running! Fred had always fantasized that, one day, Merlin would appear from nowhere and come to his rescue, teach him everything he needed to be a brilliant wizard and make all his worries go away. He never thought for one moment that he might *actually* get to meet him *in real life*.

But here was his chance. He'd enter the competition, capture the lizard's tail, meet and become friends with Merlin, learn brilliant magic and, most importantly of all, make his parents proud – and his siblings shut up. There were a handful of leaflet versions of the poster in a small plastic case underneath the main poster and Fred picked one up. Then he noticed the small print underneath the announcement:

Whitebeard Productions accepts no responsibility for any act that may endanger witches, wizards, lizards, ears, limbs, noses, little toes, little fingers, big toes, thumbs, lips, eyebrows, unibrows, that weird bit of extra skin on elbows, moustaches, toenails, etc., etc.: or that may result in humiliation, embarrassment, maiming, serious injury or the loss of dignity and/or life. Photography is strictly prohibited.

Good luck!

*Small print? More like minuscule, terrifying print*, Fred thought. Suddenly he wasn't so keen on the idea. A fire-breathing lizard had seemed manageable just a moment ago, but the loss of toenails and lips? That was almost too horrid to imagine.

The bus pulled up. Still dazed, Fred got on.

As the bus set off, Fred gazed through the window, his mind elsewhere: a messy jumble of excitement, doubt, fear and trepidation.

The bus hit a bump. It jolted Fred back to reality.

*Maybe I'll sleep on it*, he thought.

# Chapter Three

His eyes half-closed, Fred yawned before taking a bite of his toast.

'Euuurgh,' he mumbled. It was burnt. This wasn't the good start to the day or the slice of toast that he'd hoped for.

He hadn't slept. He'd been too busy tossing and turning, waking himself from nightmares about fire-breathing wizards and lizards with no toenails, eyebrows or lips. Or was it the lizards that breathed fire and the wizards who lost all their toenails? It was all a bit of a blur. All he knew was that after a restless night he'd been really looking forward to that slice of toast. And it had disappointed him almost as much as he disappointed his parents.

Fred scraped off the worst of the black layer and gave the toast to Tricky, the family's cat.

She looked up at Fred with horror, as if to say: *'How dare you? That's all you think I deserve? Shame on you. You should know better.'*

Then she took the toast anyway and enjoyed it in the garden.

That's cats for you.

Fred put the last slice of bread in the toaster. He decided he had just enough time to go to the loo, so went.

Not in the kitchen, of course. He wasn't the cat. And besides, he didn't want to ruin that last slice of toast.

It was a poor judgement. I don't mean it wasn't sensible to leave the kitchen first – that was definitely a good decision – but fate and time conspired against him, and when he returned to the kitchen, the smell of burnt toast and smoke filled the air once again.

'Bother!' shouted Fred as he tried desperately to fan smoke away from the toaster.

'What's going on here?' asked Wolf, walking into the kitchen. His twin, Wilbert, followed behind.

'Nothing,' Fred replied defensively.

'Looks like he's blown up the toaster again, Wolfie!' laughed Wilbert. 'You can't do anything right, can you, little brother?' he added unkindly.

Fred turned away. His fanning had only fuelled the fire. Little flames flickered at the top of the toaster. His brothers chuckled to each other.

'I mean, if you're struggling to deal with these tiny flames, how on earth will you get on with actual, proper fire?' Wilbert teased.

Fred froze.

'Yeah,' Wolf chipped in. 'This is a pathetic excuse for a fire. I can't imagine how you'd get on with, I don't know … say … a *terrible, fire-breathing lizard.*'

He and Wilbert pretended to roar, then fell about laughing.

'What … Where … How do you know about that?' Fred stuttered.

He'd been hoping to keep the idea to himself. He wasn't even sure he was going to go ahead with it.

'Left this lying around, didn't you?' replied Wilbert, waving the leaflet Fred had picked up from the bus stop.

Fred tried to grab it from him, but instead

lost his balance and fell over the cat, who'd returned, hoping to find another slice of incinerated toast.

'Let me look at this again,' said Wolf. 'Let's see ... "daring ... bold ... courage ... nerve ... skill". Doesn't sound much like our little Fred to me!'

'It does mention fools, though,' Wilbert chipped in, 'so he might be all right after all.'

'That's true. But then again, why would Merlin bother with someone so hopeless? Even if by some miracle you were to meet him, he'd take one look at you and give up straight away. Better things to do, I reckon.'

'Yeah,' Wilbert agreed. 'Not even a wizard as brilliant as Merlin could teach you, little bro. No wonder the teachers at school don't stand a chance!'

Fred rose to his feet but said nothing. The toaster was still smouldering away. Tricky was no longer interested in its contents.

The rest of Fred's family arrived in the kitchen for breakfast. 'Gosh! What a ghastly smell!' his dad announced.

'Oh, not *again*, Freddie!' his mother said. 'What have I told you about making toast?'

'That it's not safe,' Fred sighed in reply.

'That's right, dear. Now, let one of your brothers by so they can put out that fire,' she commanded.

Fred reluctantly moved aside. With the tiniest flick of his wand, Wilbert extinguished the fire. He looked at Fred and grinned smugly. 'Simple,' he said.

'Mum,' Wolf enquired, 'has Fred told you about his new adventure?'

*Great. Thanks, Wolf,* thought Fred.

'What adventure's this?' Fred's parents asked as one.

'It's … nothing,' Fred replied.

'Nothing?' laughed Wilbert. 'Ha!

It's anything but!'

Wilbert passed the leaflet to his parents.
They silently mouthed the words to
themselves as they read – until their mouths
dropped open in horror.

'Surely not?' Fred's father asked.

'What is it?' Willow and Wilda said, desperate to know what was so shocking.

'Well, *why* not?' Fred retaliated. Anger had sparked something inside him. He'd had enough of standing by meekly, quietly absorbing the blows to his self-worth and confidence.

His mother peered past the end of her pointy nose and over the top of the glasses resting at the end of it.

'Darling, don't you think it's a bit … advanced? Dangerous? Suicidal?'

She coughed.

'I mean to say, it sounds an awfully tricky task. If it's adventure you're after, there's a worm in the garden that's being a bit of a nuisance. You could sort that out for me. You know how I hate worms!'

'*Worms and washing-up!* That's *all* you think I can do, isn't it?!' he shouted. 'All you think about is vanish this, transform that, magic here, magic there! Wouldn't it be wonderful if poor little Fred was as *brilliant* at magic as all his *perfect* brothers and sisters? Have you ever thought there might be more to a person than simply what they can do with their wand? *Well, have you?*' he demanded.

For once, the rest of the family was silent.

'Of course you haven't,' Fred finished, 'because you never look past the ends of them, do you? Well, I'm going to show you what I can do! Though I don't know why any of you are pretending to care anyway. That lizard would be doing you a favour by gobbling me up! You could all get on with your lives without being embarrassed by me!'

'Freddie, don't say that—' his mother started.

But Fred was gone. He had to get out.

Out of the room. Out of earshot. Out of sight.

He still hadn't had any breakfast, unless you count the single bite of apocalyptic toast. But, despite what his stomach was telling him, hunger was the least of his worries …

Because he'd clearly gone mad.

He'd just agreed to face the lizard.

# Chapter Four

His stomach rumbling loudly amid the usual hubbub of break time, Fred watched nervously as Marvin read what he'd just been handed.

'Well, it's certainly an *interesting* idea,' Marvin said.

His tone didn't exactly fill Fred with

confidence. And Marvin had been staring at the leaflet for far too long.

'What is it?' Fred asked. 'You're not exactly filling me with confidence, Marv, and you've been staring at that leaflet for far too long,' he said. (See, I told you.)

'Well, it's just … it does sound rather dangerous,' said Marvin eventually.

'You don't think I can do it, either?' replied Fred, disappointed. He'd hoped his best friend would give him a boost.

'I just think you need to think about it very carefully. Are you sure it's a good idea?' he asked.

'Of course I'm not,' Fred replied in an instant. 'It's a terrible idea. Ridiculous. Probably fatal – or *worse*. You know it says I might lose my lips, right?'

Marvin grimaced.

'But what choice do I have?' Fred continued. 'I've already said I'll do it.'

'You haven't signed up yet, have you?' Marvin asked. 'It's not too late to change your mind.'

'I'm as good as signed up, as far as my family are concerned,' Fred sighed. 'And how would I look if I backed out now? Useless. Pathetic.'

Marvin gave Fred a sympathetic look.

'I'm so fed up of being a disappointment, embarrassing them all the time because my spells backfire and I can't do the simplest of magic. I sometimes think my family wishes I didn't exist. You know what they think I'm capable of? Washing-up, and talking worms out of being a nuisance! That's all!'

'Well, to be fair, you are very good at that,' Marvin said.

'What?' asked Fred. 'Washing-up? Or talking to worms?'

'Both,' Marvin said. 'And people don't realise how complicated worms can be. It's a real skill you have there, Fred.'

'Thanks … I guess,' he replied. Fred knew Marvin was trying to make him feel better, but he wasn't sure he was helping.

The friends fell silent for a while, both lost in thought.

Eventually Fred spoke.

'So, what do you think I should do?' he asked.

Marvin turned his head and stared into the distance. He seemed to be searching for the answer. Then he read the leaflet again.

'I think you should do it,' he said finally. 'It's going to be dangerous – there'll be peril, an evil monster, fire. You may well lose a limb, an eye, your dignity. Maybe even all three. Maybe worse,' he said.

'Marvin, where are you going with this?' Fred asked, with fear in his voice.

'My point is,' Marvin continued, 'life is dangerous. You might not encounter evil, fire-breathing monsters every day, but it's still dangerous. Every time you get on that bus there's danger involved – yet you still take that risk. Why not take this one? I think you need to do it – for you.'

Fred couldn't really see how his bus journeys bore any relevance to taking on an evil, fire-breathing lizard. He'd never considered his daily commute dangerous before either. Now Marvin had made it an extra thing to worry about.

'You can do this,' Marvin said. 'You can. At least, you have to *try* because if you don't, you'll forever wonder, *What if?* This is a chance to prove to yourself what you're really capable of.'

Fred nodded. Marvin knew him well.

'And *that* prize! Being taught by Merlin?' Marvin raised his eyebrows and let out a long, clear whistle that went from high to low. 'Imagine what you could learn, Fred! That's got to be worth signing up for, surely?'

Fred nodded, and his fantasy of Merlin solving all his problems appeared in his mind once again. This time, though, its happy ending was interrupted, replaced instead by the image of his brother, cackling. What was it he'd said? *'Not even Merlin could teach you!'* – that was it. Fred tried not to dwell on those words, hoping his brother, for once, was wrong about him.

'But what about the lizard, the peril and the danger, the threat to my ears and the weird bit of skin on my elbow?' Fred asked. 'I'm fond of that bit of skin. It's one of the few things I like about myself.'

'I like that about you too, Fred, everyone does,' Marvin said. 'And as for the lizard, you'll be fine. You're the bravest wizard I know!'

'Don't be silly, Marvin,' Fred laughed.

'I'm serious,' Marvin replied. 'Completely

serious. You face your fears every day by coming to school and braving what's thrown at you. And then you go home and cope with your brothers and sisters making fun of you! But you never give up. Even when you feel like you're hopeless and humiliated. *That* takes courage.'

Fred had never thought of things that way before. He was starting to feel a little bit taller, a little bit stronger, a little more confident. Talking to Marvin had been a good idea.

'Maybe you're right, Marv. But what am I going to do when – if – I'm face-to-face with that monster? We both know I'm useless at magic. I can't *wash* the lizard into submission!'

'It's not your biggest strength,' Marvin agreed, trying to spare his friend's feelings. 'But you've got to believe in yourself, Fred. If you keep telling yourself that you're useless, that's what you'll be. I know you've got it in you. You've just got to find it yourself.'

Fred blushed and didn't know where to look.

'And, anyway,' said Marvin, 'beating the lizard is going to take more than just magic. Keeping a cool head, thinking quickly, showing heart and determination. All those things will be important. You'll find a way, I know it. You've got other skills.'

'Like talking to worms?' Fred said.

'Exactly!' Marvin chuckled. 'Think of the lizard as just a slightly bigger than normal, more evil worm.'

'One that breathes fire and gobbles up wizards.' Fred gulped.

'Well, maybe don't think of it like that.'

'Got it,' said Fred.

'And don't worry about losing an ear. We can always find you another. I know a man who knows a man who knows a boy with more ears than he knows what to do with. If you lose one, he's sure to hear about it.'

# Chapter Five

A few days later, Fred found himself walking slowly in the direction of the town hall. After talking to Marvin, Fred had felt sure that he should enter the competition, but now that he was actually going to sign up, doubt and uncertainty threatened to swallow him. Was this a terrible, fatal idea? Was he doomed to fail and humiliate his family even more? What would he do if he *did* get as far as the lizard?

Then, a different thought popped into his mind. Maybe facing the lizard was what he had to do, what he needed to do. Maybe he could be as courageous as Marvin said he was. Maybe he could find a way to beat the lizard and prove to his family – to himself – that he was worth something. And Marvin was right. The biggest thing of all, the thing that would bug him for the rest of his life, was this: if he didn't sign up, he would forever wonder what might have been.

So Fred continued putting one foot in front of the other.

Outside the town hall were two burly, gnarly creatures. Both were dressed entirely in green and looked as though they'd already fought a fire-breathing lizard several times – and lost. One of them had a face covered in scars, and several boils protruded from his cheeks like disgusting baubles on the least festive Christmas tree ever imagined. The other had a grubby, slightly orange complexion, and an enormous body but unusually small head, atop of which perched a ridiculously tiny hat. It made him look as though he'd washed the hat on a very high heat but had forgotten to take it off first, so that both his headwear and head had shrunk in the wash. Judging by the vacant expression on his face, this was probably exactly what had happened.

Fred approached them, holding the leaflet.

'Hi. I'm, err, here to sign up for the competition,' he said.

'Password,' one of the doormen replied.

'Sorry?' said Fred.

'That's not the password,' said the other doorman. 'Try again.'

'I didn't know there would be a password,' Fred said, bemused.

'Nope. That's not the password either,' answered the first doorman. 'Try again.'

'Errrrmm …'

'No. That's not it,' the boily one said. 'Have another go.'

'Merlin?' Fred guessed.

'Nope.'

'Lizard?'

'Afraid not. It begins with "P",' the less warty doorman offered.

'Pterodactyl?' Fred asked.

'What?' both doormen said. 'That doesn't start with "P"'.

'I think you'll find it does,' Fred replied. 'Take a look.'

Fred flicked his wand and a dictionary appeared out of thin air. (Now, I know what you're thinking – if Fred is supposed to be rubbish at magic, how can he do such an amazing, advanced trick? Well, because summoning dictionaries is actually very basic, low-level magic, one of the first things wizards learn at school.)

The doormen flicked through the dictionary until they got to 'T'.

'Well, it's not under "T", Michael,' one

said to the other.

'That's odd,' Michael replied. 'That's where I'd expect it to be.'

'It's under "P"!' Fred said, losing patience.

Michael slowly turned to 'P'. He searched for a moment, then scratched his head.

'Well, I never!' he gasped. 'It's there! Who knew? What were we saying earlier, Terry? You learn something new every day!'

They laughed in unison.

'So can I go in?' Fred asked, frustrated.

'Pterodactyl's not the password either, I'm afraid,' Terry said. 'Even if it does start with "P". Have another go.'

'Possum?' Fred tried.

'It's not the password,' Michael said. 'But I'd sure like to know what it is!'

'It's flowers, isn't it?' Terry chipped in.

'What?' said Michael, confused.

'Terry's thinking of blossom,' Fred explained, 'which is like a possum in no way whatsoever.'

'Oh, I see,' Michael said. 'Well, anyway, the password's "Password". Can't believe you didn't get it before! Go on in.'

Fred was bewildered.

'Hang on, so you're just going to tell me the password and let me in?' he asked. 'Why have a password and waste everyone's time in the first place?'

'Well, to be honest, it makes us feel more importanter, you know?' Terry explained sadly.

'It's no life being a town hall doorman,'

Michael added. 'Anyone could do it.'

Clearly, thought Fred, as he walked past the strange creatures and into the building.

The town hall was much larger than Fred had expected and the sound of his footsteps echoed as he moved towards the back of the ornately panelled room. Given the brilliant prize on offer, he'd expected to find a long line of people waiting to sign up, so he was surprised and unnerved to find that there wasn't a queue at all. *Where is everyone?* Fred thought, before realising the likely answer: that the only wizard foolish enough to enter the competition was *him*.

On the wall at the back of the hall hung the same poster promoting the competition that Fred had first seen at the bus stop, only this one was even more enormous. It stretched from ceiling to floor so that Merlin's face and mesmerising turquoise eyes dominated the entire room. Seeing his hero staring back at him and smiling relaxed Fred a little, and gave him the courage he needed to sign up. He felt grateful there wasn't a huge picture of the lizard staring back at him; had there been, he was certain he'd immediately have turned round and gone home. Instead, he was spurred on, his dreamy mind wandering once again to the prize that awaited the winner.

Underneath Merlin's poster, sitting at a

very old and weathered desk, was an even older and more weathered wizard. He smiled warmly at Fred and shook his hand.

'Signing up for the competition, are we?' he asked.

'Seems so,' replied Fred. He still wasn't in the best of moods, given his encounter with the doormen.

'Excellent. It's a super prize, isn't it?' said the old man, noticing Fred's eyes lingering on the poster. 'I met Merlin once, you know. Charming chap. Beautiful beard. And how good of him it is to offer his time to help whomever wins this fantastic competition! Mind you, I wouldn't expect anything less of the fellow – a true gent! Now then, anyway, there are a few questions I need you to answer.

Competition entry criteria, as it were.'

He held out a scroll at arm's length above his head and let it unravel. It pooled on the floor.

'Just a few?!' Fred asked.

This was going to take for ever, and he was certain he'd fail all of them.

'Just a few,' the administrator confirmed. 'Now, let's begin.'

He looked at the scroll, then back at Fred.

'Are you a wizard?' he asked.

'Yes,' Fred replied. *That wasn't so difficult,* he thought.

'Now, this one's a bit trickier!' the old man said, and Fred's heart sank. 'Do you own a wand?'

'Yes.' Fred considered explaining that he

didn't really know how to use it, but thought better of the idea.

'Super!' the old man replied. 'Third question. Now this one really is tricky,' he said. 'So listen carefully.'

'Will do,' Fred replied.

'In 1682, the official record for the World's Heaviest, Most Orange Pumpkin was broken by a very old farmer called Ralph. Now, I'm not going to ask you how much it weighed – that would be grossly unfair! But I am going to ask you a very difficult question, I'm afraid! Think about it very carefully and take as much time as you need,' the old man advised.

'Okay,' said Fred. His pulse was racing.

'Now, here it is. Ready?'

'Yes.'

'What colour – ' he studied the scroll carefully – 'was Ralph's orange pumpkin?' The old man's face contorted into a concerned but somehow encouraging expression.

Was this a trick question? Fred took a deep breath, then gave his answer: 'Was Ralph's pumpkin … orange?'

The old man gave a delighted yelp and clapped his hands together in triumph.

'Superb!' he said. 'You are a very clever young man! That really was a very difficult question – the hardest question imaginable. Not for hundreds of years has a wizard so young answered correctly! You'll do great things, my boy! That lizard's in for quite the shock, I'd say!'

Fred thought this unlikely, but smiled nonetheless.

'Well, good luck!' the old wizard said.

'That's it?' Fred asked. 'No more questions?'

'No more,' the wizard replied. 'I said there were just a few, and just a few there were.'

'But why is the scroll so long?'

The elderly wizard turned it round to show Fred. The handwriting was enormous – the biggest Fred had ever seen. But there were only three questions on the roll of paper.

'Dear boy, when you get to my age it's a miracle to be able to see at all! I can barely make you out, let alone read normal handwriting!' he explained.

'I understand,' said Fred. 'How old are you, if you don't mind me asking?'

'I mind not at all,' the old man smiled. 'Quite the opposite. That I've made it this far is a source of great pride! Today happens to be my four hundred and seventy-third birthday,' he announced. 'I remember each and every one of them!'

'Well, a very happy birthday to you!' Fred said in amazement.

'How very kind you are,' he replied. 'Now, can I offer you one piece of advice before the competition? My four hundred and seventy-three years have taught me rather a lot, after all!'

'Please do,' Fred said.

'Get a good night's sleep!' the wizard said. 'It's

the single most important thing I've learned.'

*Ah*, Fred thought. He'd been hoping for something a little more enlightening. Something that might have helped *fight* the lizard. Something *useful*.

'Great. Thank you,' he mumbled. 'I'll do my best.'

And, carrying that sparkling pearl of immense wisdom, Fred went on his way.

# Chapter Six

Fred woke with a fright. He had the strangest feeling that he'd forgotten something.

He glanced with a bleary, half-opened eye at his bedside clock. It took a moment for his sleepy brain to process the numbers. Then he yelped. His eyes were now open wide in horror.

The clock read 10:15 a.m. It was the day of the competition and he'd slept through his alarm! He'd meant to be up hours ago.

Remarkably, despite expecting to have the same nightmare about the fire-breathing lizard and losing toenails that he'd had every night since he signed up for the competition a week before, Fred had slept like a baby. He'd not stirred all night. He even wondered whether the ancient wizard who'd signed him up to the competition had performed some sort of secret spell on him to help him sleep so spectacularly well. Yet instead of feeling rested, Fred felt rising panic. The competition was due to start at noon. The bus journey would take him an hour at least, and he was nowhere near ready to leave home.

Fred pulled himself out of bed and began hurriedly searching for his bag. Once located, he flung into it everything and anything he thought might come in useful for the day: a torch, a raincoat, a sunhat, a fresh pair of undercrackers, some string, an old conker, a family-sized bag of cheese, leek and bacon crisps which was already open, a not-so-fresh pair of undercrackers, a fascinating book about London's pigeons, two very shiny spoons and a corkscrew, his grandma's parking permit, a library card and a small but very lifelike model of the Sultan of Scarborough.

Fred wasn't sure how handy these things would turn out to be, but decided he'd rather have them and not use them than regret leaving them at home. The last

thing he wanted was to be facing the lizard desperately needing his library card, kicking himself because he hadn't packed it.

When there was no longer any room in his bag, Fred flung it over his shoulder, picked up his wand and made for the front door.

His path out of the house was blocked.

Standing in front of the exit, arms folded, was Wilbert.

'You're not *actually* going to do this, are you?' he asked in a less-than-friendly tone.

'Wilbert, haven't you got some incredibly important magic to get on with?'

Fred sighed. 'If you'd just get out of the way, that would be great, thanks!'

'Don't get sarcastic with me, little brother,' Wilbert replied coldly. 'You know none of us want you to do this.'

'And why's that?' asked Fred. He already knew the answer.

'Listen, Mum and Dad might *pretend* they don't want you to get hurt. But really we're all just worried that you'll make a mockery of us. *Yet again.*'

Fred tried not to feel hurt by his brother's comments. Though he'd heard them all before, the words still stung. But he'd had enough of hearing them, and though part of him worried his brother might be right, he felt more desperate than ever to prove him – everyone – wrong.

'Come on, Wilbert. Stop worrying!' he said with a fake laugh. 'With any luck, I'll be first in the queue and the lizard will gobble me up before anyone has the chance to notice. I'll be gone in a jiffy. Then you can all happily get on without me.'

Wilbert didn't budge.

Fred needed to think of something. There was no way he could out-muscle his older, bigger brother, nor out-magic him. Time was ticking and he was already late.

'Er, Wilbert?' he said, moving his gaze to behind his brother's shoulder. 'Whatever you do, don't move.'

'What?' Wilbert said.

'It's all right,' Fred said. 'It's not *that* big. I mean, it's pretty big, but it's not *enormous*.'

'What isn't enormous?' asked Wilbert.

'The spider. Behind you.'

'Oh, *come on*, Fred. Don't be an idiot. I'm not falling for that,' his brother huffed.

There was the tiniest hint of worry in his voice. Fred picked up on it.

'Actually, now that it's a bit closer,' Fred continued, 'it is *fairly* enormous. But don't worry, it's not *gargantuan*. It's just that … it does look quite … angry.'

'Fred. Stop it.' Wilbert trembled. However macho and fearless he tried to seem, Wilbert's biggest fear was spiders.

'Shhh!' Fred whispered. 'I think it's seen you. Just. Stay. Still.'

'Where is it? WHERE IS IT?' Wilbert squealed.

Fred pulled his wand from his bag and pointed it towards Wilbert's shoulder.

'I'm going to get rid of it,' he said, before closing his eyes and muttering an incantation he was making up on the spot. 'I just need to remember the spell.'

'Don't do that!' Wilbert shouted. 'You'll probably kill me!'

'Don't panic. I've got it,' Fred declared. 'Ready? One … two … three.'

His brother dared not risk it. He dashed as fast as he could away from the front door, Fred's wand and the enormous imaginary spider.

Fred chuckled. Even if he did get eaten up in a couple of hours' time, at least he'd die marginally happier.

'What was all that about?' said his father, who'd emerged from the kitchen clutching a half-eaten banana, taking Fred by surprise. 'Where are you off to?'

Fred's grin faded. His plan to make his exit unnoticed wasn't going very well.

'Spider,' Fred mumbled. 'And I'm just going … out.'

Fred's father's eyes lingered on Fred's backpack.

'Out, eh?' he said, before inhaling the remainder of his snack. 'And you need to take all that, do you?'

'Best be prepared,' Fred muttered. He met

his father's gaze. He knew his dad knew exactly what he was up to, but for some reason Fred was unwilling to admit the truth out loud.

Eventually his dad spoke.

'Listen, I know it's not easy for you, living in this family.' He made a vague gesture with his hands and the floppy banana skin waggled in the air. A stringy bit of peel flew off and attached itself to the wall. 'We give you a tough time sometimes—'

'Dad, honestly,

it's fine,' Fred interjected, aware of the time. A long discussion about family life was the last thing he needed right now, but his father wasn't finished.

'And I know we expect too much. It's not your fault that your magic is a little … limited. Your brothers and sisters don't help, I know—'

'Dad, please—'

'But, Fred, we're just worried. This competition, it's dangerous. And you're not the most gifted—'

'WINSTON, WHAT'S GOING ON?' Fred's mum suddenly shouted at her husband, appearing from nowhere. 'Wilbert's wailing about some humongous spider and how Fred's trying to escape and how he's going to disgrace the family and—'

'Oh,' she said, catching sight of Fred and his rucksack. 'You are trying to leave! Where are you going with all that—'

And then she remembered. About the competition, about Fred's promise to show them what he could do. About the lizard, the peril, the danger.

'Freddie, darling, we've talked about this, please—' she started, but when Fred raised his hand, signalling her to stop, she did.

'Mum. I know. You've told me so many times. I don't need to hear it again—'

'But, dear, it's dangerous—'

'I know, but—'

'And the lizard could—'

'Yes, Mum, I'm aware—'

'Son,' Fred's dad interrupted for the final time. 'The most important thing to us is that you're safe.'

'We just don't want you getting hurt, dear!' Fred's mother wailed.

'You don't have to do this, you know,' his dad told him.

His parents' pleas reminded Fred that they thought he was destined to fail, and for the briefest of moments the thought of backing out entered Fred's mind. It left as quickly as it had arrived, replaced by the promise he'd made himself: to become a better wizard and make his parents proud. In fact, the more they tried to persuade him that facing the lizard was a terrible idea, that he couldn't do it, the more determined Fred became to prove that he *could*. Giving up now – before he'd even begun – would prove his parents right and leave everything just the same.

'Thanks, Dad,' he said, 'but I do. Not for you or Mum, or Wilbert or Wolf or anyone else. Just me. I'm sorry.'

His father nodded, and though his mother seemed about to say something, no words left her lips. Together, they turned and walked down the hallway, leaving Fred to it, not wanting to see him leave.

Fred stood for a moment, realising he was alone again. He took a deep breath, then turned towards the front door. As he pulled it open, about to step outside, someone else tugged the back of his shirt.

'Hey, Fred!'

It was Wallace. He smiled, and handed his brother a perfect piece of toast.

'Breakfast,' he said. 'You can't go without it.' He smiled again. 'Good luck.'

A rush of sadness, of confusion and fear suddenly washed over Fred. He thought of the rest of his family. He wished he'd said goodbye to them, too – his sisters, even the twins.

*Maybe they will miss me after all*, he thought.

Then he closed the door behind him.

He had a bus to catch.

# Chapter Seven

'Where to, young man?' asked the bus driver.

Fred looked down at the leaflet and the instructions under the 'How to Find Us' section.

'Erm, **DEATH'S DOOR**, please,' Fred replied.

'Are you sure?' the bus driver said, surprised.

'That's what it says here,' Fred confirmed.

'Fair enough. Not a place I'd want to find myself, though! We don't stop there very often, I tell you,' the driver replied. 'Anyway, young man, one-way or return?'

Fred hesitated. Would he be coming back? He doubted it. Why waste his money on a return?

'Just one-way, I suppose,' Fred said glumly.

'Very well. A single to **DEATH'S DOOR** it is,' the bus driver replied. 'That's the most ominous ticket I've ever sold, that's for sure!' he chuckled.

Fred found a seat at the back of the bus, where he always sat on the way to school. Then he realized the bus was almost empty, and the front seats on the top deck – the best seats, normally occupied by the youngest children on the way to school – were free. He moved, making himself comfortable. If this was to be the final bus journey of his life, he was going to make sure he enjoyed it.

As the bus drove on, Fred gazed out at rolling hills and patchwork fields gently bathed in the soft morning sun. Through the window he could feel its calming warmth on his cheeks, and he closed his eyes to appreciate the feeling more. When he reopened them, the hills had become glorious mountains, the fields vast valleys. It was a beautiful journey.

When the bus eventually came to a halt, the driver called up to Fred.

'We're here, mate,' he said. '**DEATH'S DOOR**.'

'Thanks,' Fred shouted back down.

He grabbed his bag and tried to get up. His bottom took a little longer than normal to detach itself from the seat. Something was holding it back.

'Yuk,' Fred groaned.

He attempted to pick the huge mound of chewing gum off the seat of his trousers, but this was exceptionally sticky stuff, and Fred stood for a moment with his hand firmly attached to his backside. *Great,* he thought, *not only will the lizard eat me whole, now he'll do it laughing, too.*

Eventually, after contorting himself into strange positions and lots of yanking of his hand with his free arm, Fred detached the gum from his bottom. He could feel the worry building inside him.

Saying goodbye to the driver, Fred stepped off the bus into the village of **DEATH'S DOOR**. He was surprised – a little amused even, despite his worries – to find that it was quite unlike its name suggested and not at all what he had imagined. He'd expected to arrive in a dreary, soulless, colourless place where the atmosphere was tense and ominous. In every nightmare he'd had about the competition, he'd struggled to find his way through an impossible labyrinth of miserable grey buildings, running along the same streets over and over, before the lizard finally caught up with him, roared fire and the dream ended.

Instead, the reality was a bustling village of jolly, brightly coloured higgledy-piggledy

PAPERCLIP MUSEUM
THIS WAY

buildings that lined the winding, cobbled lanes. Above the heads of friendly locals and happy visitors hung decorative bunting that depicted Merlin's smiling

CONTINUE TO MONKEY
SANCTUARY

face and added to the festival atmosphere. Helpful signs in the shape of arrows littered every street corner and the smell of delicious freshly baked goods lingered invitingly in the air. Everyone seemed relaxed, quite unfazed that somewhere, not far away, dwelled a hungry, terrifying monster. Everyone except Fred, that is, whose nervous mind was very much occupied with thoughts of the lizard.

COMPETITION START
POINT 800M FROM HERE

Above the chitter-chatter of pedestrians, he could already hear the fanfare and commotion of the competition's opening ceremony. Heart pounding faster, he followed the signs and direction of the noise.

As Fred navigated his way along the winding streets, he felt the atmosphere around him changing. The further he travelled from the cheerful village centre, the more open the landscape became, until there were only a few scattered buildings,

and the peaks of mountains, not rooftops, dominated the skyline. The air felt charged with a strange kind of nervous tension that Fred could feel affecting him, too. When he passed the last building and turned the final corner, Fred could barely believe his eyes.

In front of him was a mighty gathering of wizards and witches, the like of which he'd never seen. The sheer number of people was astounding. How silly of him to assume it was a local event: he'd expected to find a

hundred or so witches and wizards, not hundreds of thousands of them! Fred realized that the posters advertising the event must have been displayed in places all over the world. As he walked, he overheard several witches and wizards discussing all manner of tactics and techniques that they hoped, this year, would help them defeat the lizard:

'My giant feather duster didn't work as well as I'd hoped,' one wizard was saying, 'so I won't be trying *that* again.'

'You mean to say the lizard *isn't* ticklish?' his friend asked.

'Not in the slightest.'

'Right. Well, that scuppers my plans. Better think of something else. I wonder if boring it to death will work? Ha, I could read it your latest book, Nigel!'

'Lay off it!' Nigel replied. 'It's not *that* bad. Anyway, I got quite far using my fishing equipment last year. I just need to be a little more precise ...'

'I think humour's the way forward,' a witch in a separate conversation piped up. 'After I've told all my jokes, that lizard will be dying with laughter!'

'Ooooh, good idea!' her friend said excitedly. 'Are you going to tell that one about the cauldron and the cauliflower?'

'Come on, Jane – that won't cut it!' the witch replied. 'I was going to finish with the one about the griffin, the goat and the three goblins.'

'Really?' she gasped. 'But it's so *rude*!'

'Not as rude as the one you told at Margaret's funeral. That was shocking!'

Wizards and witches of every age, shape and size, of every nationality and race, were here at **DEATH'S DOOR**. They wore all manner of dress: old-fashioned, traditional magical attire; everyday clothes that non-wizards wore; outfits that were ridiculous, breathtaking or comical. Together, the colours were majestic, and as wizards moved here and there they seemed to create a human kaleidoscope. The poster had promised '*the best competition*', and with this number of wizards and witches and the impressive backdrop of mountains framed by a blue, cloudless sky, Fred was starting to see why.

Still, despite the impressiveness of it all,

the size of the gathering made his heart sink. What chance did he have against all this competition? He might as well give up now and go home.

But as soon as the thought came into Fred's head, it was knocked out again by the trembling earth beneath his feet. *What was that*? Everyone else had noticed it too. Witches exchanged worried glances. Some of the older, less sturdy wizards were knocked off their feet.

The tremors continued, more powerful each and every time. It was as if an angry giant was stomping his monstrous feet, hitting the surface of the earth in a tantrum of mighty force.

Fred reached out to grab something – anything – to steady himself. His hand clasped itself round a thin, wispy material. He fell to the ground, pulling with him the beard he'd grabbed on to, along with its frail owner.

Neither the man nor the beard was remotely impressed.

For a moment, the earth stopped shaking. Fred rose to his feet and lifted the old wizard up by way of apology. The elderly man straightened his beard, gave Fred a cursory nod, and wandered off to find a safer spot where his facial hair could get on with growing longer and more ridiculous in peace.

Then it happened.

Without a moment's notice, the air crackled, then seemed to split in two as a thunderous roar punished the atmosphere and all those gathered inside it.

In the distance, enormous flames burst into the air, singeing the clouds that had appeared out of nowhere. The roar echoed among the surrounding mountains. They seemed to shrink in fear of the sound.

The lizard had announced its presence.

# Chapter Eight

Fred stood, frozen on the spot, as all manner of panic broke out. Terrified wizards and witches fled in all directions. The frantic, desperate clicking of fingers caused a snappy chorus of its own, and the sound jolted Fred from his temporary stupor. He looked around to see many competitors vanish in a flash; others were clicking their fingers without success, terror preventing their magic from working. Dumbfounded, they simply ran away as fast as they could or tried to find somewhere to hide. *Not a bad idea*, Fred thought.

One extraordinarily rotund wizard was attempting to hide behind a tiny witch half his size; when she noticed and took offence at this, the fat wizard simply stepped to one

side and held his wand upright in front of him, as if hiding behind a minuscule tree. Fred watched as a middle-aged witch with long, luminous pink hair looked left, then right, then pulled her hair forward and down so that it covered her face and eyes, clearly believing that if she couldn't see the lizard then the lizard couldn't see her. Meanwhile, an elderly, smartly dressed wizard decided that a classic, tried-and-tested hiding place would serve best, and quickly and calmly conjured from thin air some chic gingham curtains. He appeared pleased with his choice, grinning contentedly before casually taking shelter behind them, apparently unconcerned that his shoes were visible beneath the makeshift hideout, or that his random drapery looked completely out of place making him an even more obvious target than before. Other competitors hid behind giant boulders, hoping they were out of sight and range of the lizard and its fiery breath.

All the good spots seemed to be taken. Fred watched in horror as the lizard, now fully out of its cave, rampaged through the valley. It turned its enormous head left and right to survey the scene, its thick, bulky neck stretching with the effort. Taut, hefty muscles rippled along its hulking body as it made sudden changes of direction, and its long, forked tongue – a magnificent shade of blue – flicked in and out of its mouth, dislodging disgusting globules and sticky strings of saliva from the edges of its jaw in excited anticipation of its next feast. A powerful, pointed tail whipped the ground as it went, and its muscular, sharp-clawed limbs kicked away boulders as if they were peas.

Fred looked around again, feeling the panic rise inside him. Along the craggy mountainside were dark hollows large enough to hide a person, and Fred could just about make out the figures of a few wizards who'd chosen to shelter there. It wasn't the perfect spot: if the lizard turned in the right direction, they'd surely be seen. But he couldn't see another option, and it would be better than staying where he was – out in the open, exposed, like a tasty canapé.

Heart racing, Fred scrambled across the valley, scraping shins, knees, fingers and elbows as he went. The ground was shaking beneath him again, the lizard's heavy feet bruising the valley floor with each step. Its tail swept away rocks, boulders, and wizards and witches with violent swipes. It paused for a moment, looming menacingly in the distance, as if wondering what to demolish next.

Fred was almost at the mountainside. He could see the hollow more clearly now. It was big enough for him, and maybe one other. It was deep and dark, too – the dark would hide him from sight. He was going to make it, so long as the lizard didn't turn his—

Fire surged in Fred's direction. He dived forward, body crashing into jagged boulders, bouncing then crumpling to the valley floor. The scorching heat stole his breath. He felt as if he was melting from the inside: his throat, his lungs, dry and seared. He tried to breathe, but choked. He longed for cool air, air that could soothe and replenish him.

But no.

The air was burnt and blackened, charred like the rocks around him.

*This is it*, Fred thought. *The End.*

# Chapter Nine

Fred lay motionless and confused, his eyes closed. Was he dead? He didn't feel dead, but how could he *not* be? The fire had been so close he'd felt like he was in it, burning, unable to breathe. The last thing he remembered was hitting the rock, everything turning black, and feeling as though all the air had been sucked from the atmosphere, away from him. Yet if he was thinking all this – remembering things – surely he *must* be alive. He was too scared to move or try to open his eyes, in case he found that he couldn't, because he was in fact dead. Eventually he realized how silly it was to just lie there wondering, and that he might as well find out. When he tried to wiggle his toes and they moved as normal, Fred was filled with relief. He *wasn't* dead. Not yet, anyway. Despite the raging inferno around him, the flames had missed him by centimetres. He wasn't on fire. He was lucky.

Fred opened his eyes and looked around. He could still see a clear path towards the opening of the hiding place. He couldn't tell if the lizard had seen him or was just spraying fire at random, but he didn't want to hang around to find out. Gathering himself, Fred glanced over his shoulder. The lizard was looking the other way. This was his chance.

Just then, the creature roared a raspy, penetrating roar. Fred knew what was coming next. As fast as he could, he crawled the remaining few metres to the hollow, keeping low. He heard the lizard inhale deeply, then blast another fiery wave in his direction.

Fred flung himself into the tiny cave. As the fire surged towards him, its heat dislodged the mountainside and hot shards of rock splintered in all directions, huge lumps falling to the ground with a thump. One fell in front of the entrance to Fred's cave a split second before the fire reached him; he was plunged into near total darkness, but also blocked from view and the flames. Through the small slither at the hollow's entrance he could still feel the deathly heat, but for now, he was safe.

Exhausted, Fred collapsed against the cold, hard rock of the cave.

*What am I doing?* he thought. *WHAT AM I DOING?! I'm a moron, an idiot. I could be at home, warm and cosy. Miserable, hopeless, a disappointment, yes — but still warm and cosy. Better than being frightened to death, stuck in a cave, hungry.*

Then he remembered!

He opened his now slightly chargrilled backpack and pulled out the enormous packet of crisps he'd hastily packed that morning. He hadn't realized how old they were: the use-by date had long been and gone. The crisps must have been festering on his bedroom floor for months. Still, the bag was almost full and he was grateful to have something to eat. He prodded a crisp: it was soft in the middle, but its edges had been nicely crisped up again by the heat of the lizard's fire. He sniffed it: not *revolting*. It survived the lick test, too. Fred ate it, then scoffed a whole handful in a blur, being careful to save some for later just in case. Slightly soggy, dusty, two-year-old bacon, leek and cheese crisps had never tasted so good.

As he chewed, Fred weighed up his options. He couldn't see how winning this competition would be worth all the terror he'd have to go through to do it. Facing that lizard? Now that he'd actually seen it, the thought sent shivers from his ears to his toes. Not even a lesson with Merlin was worth that risk. Those wizards and witches who'd already made their escape clearly agreed.

Yet, he *still had* both his ears and all his toes. He hadn't lost his lips and his favourite bit of elbow-skin was just about intact. Better, more accomplished magicians had vanished, fled, hidden or been eaten up with ease, but he was still alive, heart beating, lungs breathing.

He wasn't defeated yet.

For a while, Fred could still hear cries outside and the lizard's roar, so he tiptoed back to the slim gap in the entrance to the cave and peered through. A few brave and hardy witches and wizards were obviously taking the fight to the lizard, not prepared to give up on the prize on offer just yet. They cast huge nets and ropes and spears and missiles from their wands; some conjured great walls and rivers of water to tackle the beast's breath; others attempted to confuse the lizard by disguising themselves or creating illusions. Spell after spell was launched at the creature: many missed their target and died in the air; others rebounded off rocks, causing everyone to dive to avoid them; and some hit their mark, but to no avail. The fearsome creature barely noticed it had been hit; its tough, armour-like skin was too thick to penetrate. The few witches and wizards who were foolish enough to let their concentration slip, and took their eyes off the monster for more than a second, paid the ultimate fiery price. Fred couldn't watch any longer.

Gradually, as an hour or two crawled past and those still fighting began to lose their will, both sounds faded. Eventually, they stopped completely. An eerie silence trickled into the cave.

Fred walked back to the entrance and peered out into the valley once more. He was dreading going back out there, into the unknown, unsure whether the lizard lurked unseen behind a wall of rock or round a hidden corner. But he had no choice. There was nothing to be gained by hiding in a cave for the rest of his life, other than a covering of moss and mould, perhaps. The small gap was just big enough for him to squeeze through. Heart pounding, legs trembling, he stepped outside.

Steam and smoke hung in the air. Flames still flickered from the valley floor. Fred, as far as he could tell, was completely alone. Though he could see bodies around him, none of them moved.

Fred strained his eyes again, searching for a tail, a sudden trail of fire, a glint of scaly skin. The lizard was nowhere to be seen.

This was his opportunity to leave, to go

home – to be safe.

But he couldn't do it. Something was keeping him there, forcing him to stay. Voices fought in his head. One screamed at him to leave, forget the lizard, save himself, that he wasn't good enough and couldn't do it. But another voice – a strange but forceful mixture of Marvin's and his own – shouted back. It told him to stay, to prove people wrong – to prove *himself* wrong. *Believe in yourself. It's about more than just magic.*

Fred knew then that he wasn't finished.

He had to find the lizard.

# Chapter Ten

Fred started to move cautiously across the valley, looking for any signs of the creature.

The ground was still roasting hot and he could feel the soles of his shoes starting to melt in the heat. He quickened his pace, skipping between boulders and deep craters created in the earlier mayhem.

His heart raced. His senses were alert, on edge. Waiting for the lizard to emerge at any moment, ready to eat him whole or roast him there and then.

As Fred moved forward, a thought struck him: *the craters*. They weren't *just* craters. They were too orderly, too similar. They appeared one after the other, slightly to the left, then slightly to the right.

These were footprints. Giant, terrifying footprints. Footprints that belonged to the lizard.

Fred followed them closely. Now, as far as he could see, he was the only wizard around.

It was just him and the lizard, wherever it was. Soon it would just be the lizard, he worried. All the doubts he'd managed to banish just moments before swallowed him again: *Give up. Go home and have a cup of tea. All the other wizards have perished or given up, so what chance do you have?* He could feel the panic wash over him, causing his stomach to knot and his chest to tighten. He suddenly felt very lonely.

The footprint craters came to an end. Fred raised his gaze from the ground to the mouth of the cave that now lay in front of him. He crept a little closer.

He could hear a deep, steady, rumbling

sound, which drowned out the sound of his own heavy breaths. He felt the ground vibrating beneath his feet, reminding him of just how enormous the beast really was. A shudder ran down Fred's spine. Each of his senses seemed heightened, and he could smell the charred rock and burnt soil, victims of the monster's anger.

He stood at the side of the cave, wanting to peer in but fearful of being seen by the lizard. Struck by an idea, Fred took off his backpack and reached inside, pulling out the two spoons. Using the gum he'd saved from the bus journey he fixed the spoons together by their handles, so the two round spoon heads were now at either end of a new, longer implement. He breathed on the shinier of the two, then buffed it with his shirt until it was polished enough to show his reflection. Bending it slightly, he leaned against the rock at the edge of the cave's entrance, before holding his makeshift tool at arm's length in front of him. Fred carefully angled the spoon until he found the perfect position to see the inside of the cave reflected on its metal surface.

Craning his neck, he saw in the spoon the huge, scaly body rising and falling with each breath the monster took. There, inside the cave, the lizard lay, deeply asleep. It snored away happily, its belly full of magic and the wizards and witches it had greedily gobbled up for lunch.

Fred slumped down against the outside of the cave, needing to think. It quickly dawned on him that he hadn't a clue what to do next. He hadn't planned this bit of his adventure: in fact, he hadn't planned any of it.

For all the hours he'd spent thinking about the lizard and the competition, he'd never considered how he'd actually come away with its tail. Yet there it was, staring him in the face. He'd got much further than he'd ever thought possible. He wished he could just yank it off and walk out of the cave, that it could be as easy as that. But it couldn't. He'd have to slice it off, and there was nothing in his backpack sharp enough to cut off the lizard's tail. Using his wand would be useless: he didn't know how to conjure a knife nor use magic to cut things. And anyway, any such attempt was bound to wake the lizard and result in certain death. Fred didn't much fancy the *possibility* of death, let alone the *certainty* of it.

The harder Fred thought, the further away the answer seemed, and he realized just how stupid he'd been. What on earth was he going to do? There wasn't a spell in the wizarding world that could help him. Well, at least not one that he could do. It was hopeless. How foolish he'd been to think there was even the tiniest chance that he might pull it off; that he, a small eight-year-old boy, useless at magic, could outperform experienced, talented witches and wizards and outwit the beast they'd succumbed to. Fred thought of his brothers and Marvin and envied them more than ever: they'd know what to do, what magic to use. How he longed to be a proper wizard, with tricks up his sleeve that he could actually perform.

With a numb bottom and knees that were aching from sitting awkwardly for so long, Fred eventually realized that he had no choice but to head inside and hope for the best. He needed the tail, the prize, the tuition from Merlin. It was his only hope of getting better at magic. He'd have to improvise, to come up with a plan as he went. There was nothing else for it. He pushed himself off the floor. He took several long, deep breaths to compose himself and slow his racing heart.

Cautiously – nervously – he entered the cave.

Fred snuck as quietly as he could past the sleeping lizard's head. It was the last place he wanted to be if the beast suddenly woke up. He didn't really want to be near its tail either: one swipe from that would finish him off. He settled on lingering near its middle, the least dangerous part he could think of.

Then, out of desperation and not knowing what else to do, Fred searched inside his backpack again for anything that might help. He removed the items one by one. He slipped the torch into his pocket, but didn't dare turn it on for fear of waking the monster. He piled the raincoat, sunhat and pants neatly to one side: he couldn't see a use for them. He placed the packet of crisps on top.

The library card was a waste of space, and so, too, was his gran's parking permit: he couldn't see how they could help him one bit. The book about pigeons was an enchanting page-turner, but other than entertaining Fred for a few minutes it would be no use at all. The rest of the items were no better, although Fred thought that the statue of the Sultan of Scarborough would work nicely as a way to spruce up the cave a bit.

Surely there had to be *something* he could use? He turned the bag upside down and shook it gently.

Out bounced the conker. It echoed through the cave.

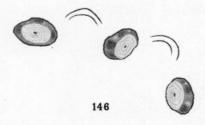

'Don't wake up! Don't wake up!' Fred begged the lizard under his breath, as he chased after the conker as quietly as he could. Towards the back of the cave he finally managed to dive on top of it and smother the noise of its bounces.

The lizard grunted loudly. Fred kept as still as a statue. The lizard shuffled a little, its great tail shifting from one side of its body to the other. It remained asleep. Fred breathed a huge sigh of relief.

As he rose to his feet, he spotted something glistening in the tiny beam of light that shone through a crack in the ceiling of the cave. Fred bent down and studied it. He ran his fingers along its smooth, beautiful surface. He picked it up, needing both his arms and all his might to bear its weight. He couldn't help but smile.

In his hands, perfectly preserved, was a section of glorious, shiny tail: a tail that the lizard had shed.

Fred couldn't believe his luck. He placed the tail carefully back on the ground, silently repacked his backpack and flung it over his shoulder. He needed to get away fast, before the lizard woke up. He picked up the tail again and made for the cave entrance.

His arms burned under the tail's weight, his legs buckling under the strain. This was going to be harder than he thought.

As he readjusted his hold, a heavy, clumsy, shuffling sound stopped him in his tracks. Fred looked behind him.

Two marbled, lava-like, golden eyes flashed back at his own, and as their gazes met, the lizard's black, vertical pupils seem to sharpen with excitement. It blinked, as if to check it was fully awake and seeing correctly. Then it opened its powerful jaws, wide enough for Fred to sneak a peek at what was sure to be his final resting place.

Fred considered fleeing, but he knew it was futile. He couldn't outrun the lizard or its ferocious breath.

This time, it really was *it*.

Fred braced himself. He closed his eyes and hid his face behind his raised arm as if this would somehow offer some protection against what was to come.

He stood there waiting.

Waiting for his short, unfulfilled little life to come to a horrible end …

# Chapter Eleven

Fred waited for what felt like an eternity.

Thoughts of his family, and of Marvin, rushed through his mind.

Still he waited.

And waited.

And waited some more.

But the end he was expecting never came –

not by fire, nor by teeth, nor by tail.

Confused, Fred lowered his arm and opened his eyes.

He hadn't been waiting that long at all. The lizard's mouth was wide open, but its head was tilted back on the end of its neck. It was still yawning.

**'AAAAUUUUUUGHHHHHHHH!**

I'm so sleepy! *That* was a full-on morning.'

Fred wasn't sure if the lizard had seen him or not. He couldn't see how it hadn't, but began tiptoeing quietly backwards anyway, trying to make his escape.

'Where do you think you're going with *that*, young man?' the lizard said.

*Ah*, thought Fred. *It has seen me.*

He considered making up some elaborate lie, but in his panic his mind was working too slowly. In the end he decided to be honest.

'Well, actually, I was hoping you'd let me borrow it?' he said, nodding at the tail, trying to sound calm. 'You don't need it, do you?'

The lizard stared at him, curious.

'I don't suppose I do,' it said, 'but that's beside the point. You're trespassing!'

'Oh. Yes. I suppose I am. I'm dreadfully sorry about that,' Fred replied, before adding politely: 'Do you get many visitors?'

The lizard seemed taken aback by the question, which was understandable. Enormous, fire-breathing lizards aren't usually asked many questions.

'No,' the lizard replied. 'I rarely see anybody, to be honest. Except for this time of year when you lot arrive in town and cause me lots of bother. Still, it could be worse. Eating your sort gives me a nice change from my usual diet – and you look like you'll taste just as good as the others.'

Fred couldn't say whether or not he'd be tasty, but didn't want the lizard to find out. He tried to keep the questions going.

'Your usual diet?' Fred enquired. 'What do

you normally eat?'

'To tell you the truth, it's pretty barren round here, so whatever I can get my teeth into,' said the lizard, his tongue flicking out of his mouth and along his lips. 'If it's a bad week, mainly broccoli, turnips, kale. A goat, if I'm lucky. And I'm partial to the occasional pigeon.'

Fred spotted his chance to keep the conversation flowing.

'Funny you should mention pigeons,' he said, reaching into his backpack. 'I've brought something I think you might like.'

He chucked *Pigeons of London: A Lonely Anorak's Guide* towards the lizard's front claws.

'It's a real page-turner,' Fred said.

'Although the man who wrote it probably has a few issues.'

To Fred's despair, the lizard barely looked at the book. Instead, he ate it.

'Not much of a reader, then?' Fred asked.

'Oh, I like reading. I just prefer eating. And I've already read that book,' the lizard explained. 'You're right, though – it was most enchanting. I've never been to London. Sounds like an interesting place.'

Fred was delighted that he hadn't yet been eaten, but could sense the end of the conversation coming. He scrabbled in his backpack for something else with which to distract the lizard.

'I tell you what – why don't you take this?' he said, handing over his library card. 'That way, if you're ever in London, you can borrow some books you haven't read before.'

The lizard took the card. Fred felt its fiery gaze burning down upon him.

'And you might as well have this too,' Fred continued, donating his gran's parking permit. He was desperate to do anything and everything to keep the lizard happy, even if it meant getting in to trouble with his gran. He could deal with that later. For now, he had to get his priorities straight. 'London's great, but finding a parking space is a nightmare.'

Pleased with how quickly he'd thought on his feet, Fred let a little smile spread across his face. But the lizard was still

eyeing him suspiciously, and Fred's stomach rolled over.

'You're very generous, aren't you?' the lizard probed. 'But I'm wondering why. Are you wasting my time? Tell me again why I shouldn't just gobble you up.'

Fred thought this was a very reasonable question. He paused, considering his response carefully, then replied with the only answer he could think of.

'Well, you seem like a very nice lizard,' he said. 'You've been so kind to me so far, what with letting me in your cave and not eating me or setting me on fire. You know, you lizards get a bad reputation – monstrous, evil, terrifying, that sort of thing – but I'm sure you're all really very kind. Honestly, I wouldn't want to disappoint you as I'm sure I taste horrid.'

'Disappoint me?' the lizard asked. 'Nonsense! You look delicious and just what I fancy for pud!'

'Really?' Fred said. 'There's not much of me. I guess I'll taste just like the other wizards and witches. Except less magical, because I'm rubbish at magic, and bonier, because – well – I'm bony.'

The lizard looked Fred up and down. Fred gulped … and then an idea struck him.

'Anyway, wouldn't you like to try something different for dessert?' he continued. He hadn't a clue whether his plan would work, but couldn't see any other way out. It had to be worth a try.

The lizard sounded interested. 'Something different?' he asked.

'Yes,' said Fred. 'Something new! Do you like trying new things?'

'I'm open to it,' the lizard replied. 'What are you offering?'

'How do you feel about bacon?' Fred enquired.

'It's marvellous,' replied the lizard, 'particularly with avocado. But I've had it a million times. It's not new.'

'Well, what about leeks?' Fred offered.

'I do like leeks,' the lizard said. 'My mother used to fry them in lots of butter and it always smelled delicious. But they're not new either. You are wasting my time, aren't you?'

Fred's stomach flipped with fear. This was

proving to be a risky idea.

'I wouldn't dream of it,' he promised the lizard, trying to steady his voice. 'Have you ever had cheese?'

'Old!' the lizard shouted.

'Crisps?' Fred asked desperately. 'You must like crisps?'

'Give me something new, or I'm going to gobble you up!' the lizard roared.

Fred shakily opened his backpack. He searched inside for the only item that just might save the day.

He held it out for the lizard to sniff.

'I present to you,' he said grandly, 'bacon, leek and cheese crisps!'

The lizard leaned its nose into the packet. It slowly inhaled the stale, soggy aroma.

Then it stared directly into Fred's eyes.

'This …' it said slowly, 'is … *new*.'

A grin spread across its face.

'And I like it.'

Fred, as relieved as it is possible to be, tipped the remaining crisps into the lizard's grateful mouth.

Eager to seal the deal and get away, he added, 'Pleasure doing business with you.'

'Likewise,' the lizard mumbled through its

mouthful of crisps. 'I'm impressed – you're braver and smarter than you look, young man. In fifty years of trying, no witch or wizard has ever captured my tail. You know what – keep it. It's worth more to you than to me.'

'Thank you,' Fred smiled, struggling to believe his luck. Then, worried his good fortune could last no longer, he turned round, picked up the tail, and fled as fast as his tired little legs would carry him.

# Chapter Twelve

The joy that Fred had felt in the cave started to disappear with every step he took towards the finish line. He was sure that at any moment his luck would run out. Despite the heavy evidence weighing down his tired arms, he couldn't believe he'd come away with the lizard's tail! He was aware of the sensations in his body – the hot, uneven ground under his feet, sweat trickling down his forehead and back, the burning muscles in his legs and torso screaming in protest at him – but he felt light-headed, his mind detached from the rest of him, as if he was watching himself from above. He kept looking behind, nervous, expecting the lizard to re-emerge, demanding its tail back or another packet of crisps. But it didn't, and the adrenaline surging through Fred's body forced his feet to keep moving forward, as did his nervous, intense excitement at the prospect of finally meeting Merlin, his hero.

Gradually, the finish line got ever nearer, until it was close enough for Fred to finally see properly. A huge gathering of people was there, framed against the village's colourful buildings on the distant horizon. They waved at him, willed him on and cheered his name, grateful and relieved to see another survivor of the competition return safely to them.

He was within a stone's throw of the finish when he heard a cry of surprise as one of the spectators noticed the object he was dragging behind him.

'I don't believe it!' cried the witch. 'Look! That little wizard did it!'

The rest of the crowd noticed too and gasped in shock. Then they began to whoop and applaud. It was a wonderful, joyous sound, one that Fred had never heard before, not like this, anyway – people cheering for him. He'd done it! A mix of relief and pride

washed over him, and Fred allowed himself to enjoy the moment. His eyes flicked between the faces in the crowd. Everyone was there: the competition officials; wizards and witches who'd fled from the carnage but stayed at a distance to see what unfolded; those who had turned up only to watch; the doormen from the town hall and the elderly wizard now a week into his four hundred and seventy-fourth year; and, at the very front of the crowd, were Fred's family and Marvin. They beamed at him, cheering most loudly, leading the applause.

Suddenly it was all too much for Fred. Tired and breathless, he fell to the ground. Limbs splayed on either side of him, his eyes closed and his head began to spin. His world turned black. Everything was quiet.

The cheering stopped. The applause finished. A worried hush engulfed the crowd and Fred's family gathered round his lifeless body. His younger sisters were holding hands, his brothers linking arms, and his parents huddled together – his father, head bowed solemnly, clutching on to Fred's mother, steadying her as she sobbed.

Marvin rushed to Fred and knelt beside him. He gently shook his friend, trying to bring him round, hoping that his advice hadn't led to the worst outcome for poor Fred.

Fred didn't stir.

Marvin shook him harder. '*Please*, Fred. Come on,' he begged.

Still nothing.

Wallace joined Marvin's side and tried to wake his brother. One by one, the rest of Fred's family crouched beside him, desperately willing him to open his eyes.

His mother's sobs grew louder and louder.

His father's head stayed bowed.

Fred's siblings clutched each other, burying their heads in each other's necks. *How could they have been so mean?* they thought. They'd give anything to bring their brother back.

Lost in their grief, they didn't see Fred's lips twitch, or hear his mumbled words.

But someone from the crowd did.

'He's trying to speak!' they shouted. 'Look!'

Fred's lips twitched again, and this time Marvin saw.

'Fred! Fred, can you hear me?' he asked.

Fred mumbled something that Marvin couldn't understand.

'Say it again, I can't hear you,' Marvin told him.

Fred summoned all the effort he had left.

'I did it,' he said feebly. 'Marvin, I did it!'

Marvin smiled the happiest smile he'd ever smiled in his life.

'What did I tell you, Fred?! I knew you could!'

He helped his friend sit up, then pulled him into the biggest hug ever witnessed in **DEATH'S DOOR**.

When Marvin finally released him, Fred turned to his family.

They returned his gaze with a mixture of guilt, sadness, joy and love. His mother opened her mouth to speak, but no words came out.

Fred broke the silence.

'Told you I'd show you,' he smiled, before telling his version of events to everyone in the crowd that had eagerly gathered round to listen.

Not knowing whether to laugh or cry, Fred's family did a mixture of both. His sisters hugged him until he was almost squeezed to death and his mother showered his face with kisses until it was red with her bright lipstick.

'You had us worried for a minute there, mate,' Wallace said, ruffling Fred's hair.

'You were amazing, Freddie!' Willow and Wilda said together.

'Son, you did us proud. Did *yourself* proud,' his father said. 'We should never have doubted you. And your brothers have something they'd like to say.'

Fred turned to face the twins. He could see the guilt and remorse in their expressions.

'I'm sorry, Fred,' Wolf began. 'So, so sorry. For how I've treated you, how mean I've been.'

'Me too,' Wilbert nodded in agreement. 'We've been horrid, Fred. And you've proved us wrong. You were incredible.'

'I know we probably don't deserve it, but

can you forgive us?' they said together.

Fred looked at his brothers, smiled and then offered an outstretched hand.

'Of course,' he said. 'We're brothers, aren't we?'

The twins returned Fred's smile, but didn't shake his hand. Instead, they pulled him into a giant hug.

# Chapter Thirteen

Merlin addressed the crowd. Everyone stood attentively, gazing back at him with awe.

His wise, dazzlingly turquoise eyes shone out from the stage. They met Fred's, and a kind smile spread across his face. He winked at the young wizard. Fred felt a happy warmth rush over him.

After adjusting the brim of his purple hat, the old wizard stroked his magnificent white beard that glistened in the afternoon light. He cleared his throat. Finally, the old wizard spoke:

'Today we have witnessed something quite remarkable. Something just as magnificent and spellbinding as the greatest magic this world has ever seen. A true triumph. For today we have seen courage overcome fear, seen spirit conquer doubt, and witnessed hope vanquish despair. A young wizard, undervalued and trodden down, has proven to us all the power of endeavour, of determination, of the desire to prove one's worth and to chase one's dreams. He's reminded us of the most important principles we should hold steady in our hearts. And finally, he's shown to us the power of compromise, negotiation, and the value, in tricky times, of bacon, leek and cheese flavoured crisps.'

The crowd cheered with delight. They lifted Fred up, allowing him to surf on a wave of hands towards the stage.

The legendary wizard embraced his young admirer, and presented him with a trophy: a golden wand and half a lizard's tail.

Fred smiled warmly out at the crowd, secretly thinking to himself just how naff the trophy looked.

But it didn't matter. He felt happy.

Merlin whispered in his ear.

'You should be very proud, Fred. What you've achieved is very special. Being a wizard is about more than wandcraft and magic tricks. It's about being brave and clever and thinking on your feet. You've proved that to all of us today. I hope you realize what a marvellous young wizard you really are.'

'Thanks, Merlin,' Fred smiled. 'I think I'm beginning to.'

'I'm looking forward to our lesson, you know. Perhaps you can teach me a thing or two!' Merlin said kindly.

'I doubt it,' Fred laughed. 'But who knows what might happen.'

* * * * * *

When the ceremony was over, after he'd shaken hands with his new admirers in the crowd, posed for photos, retold his story until his lips moved independently of his brain, Fred finally rejoined Marvin and his family. It was the closest they'd been for as long as any of them could remember.

'Right, then,' Fred's father said, looking up at the darkening sky. 'We'd better be getting home. What time's your bus, Fred? We'll come back with you.'

Fred smiled. 'It's okay,' he said. 'You go on home. Marv will keep me company.'

'You sure?' Fred's mother asked.

'Sure.'

'See you at home, then,' Wilbert said.

'See you.'

Fred's family clicked their fingers and vanished as one.

As the two best friends walked to the bus stop, Fred suddenly remembered: he hadn't bought a return ticket. He hadn't believed he would be coming back.

'Err, Marv,' he asked, frustrated, 'can I borrow some money? I need another bus ticket.'

'Of course,' his friend replied. 'Hang on, I'll find you some change.'

'Thanks. Mine fell out of my pockets during the competition. With all the scrambling around it disappeared just like that,' Fred explained, clicking his fingers.

And, for the first time ever, quite to his surprise, Fred vanished into thin air, arriving home a moment later.

Marvin stopped searching for change, and laughed. He clicked his fingers and disappeared, too.

That night, Fred lay on his bed. He felt exhausted from the competition and his body ached all over, but despite his best efforts his mind just wouldn't switch off. He kept reliving the day's events: his panic at waking up late; his family's attempts to talk him out of leaving; the beautiful but nervous bus journey to **DEATH'S DOOR**; his first, terrifying sight of the lizard, the feel of its tail, the strange conversation in the cave; the relief, joy and wonder he'd felt at finishing safely and, of course, meeting Merlin, his – and *everyone's* – hero. For what felt like the first time in his life he was looking forward to seeing what his future might bring. As he stared up at the ceiling, he smiled.

How strange it was to think that when he'd woken this morning in this very same bed he hadn't known whether he'd ever lie in it again. How strange to think that he'd bought a one-way ticket because he'd thought he wouldn't need the bus ride home – and then it turned out to be true, but for a very different reason! And it hadn't been a fluke! He'd tried a few more times, just to be sure: now he really *could* travel by clicking his fingers! For the first time, Fred actually felt excited by magic now that he had his lesson with Merlin to look forward to.

*Yes*, Fred thought as he closed his sleepy eyes, it has been a very strange day indeed. Very strange – but *very* magical.

# FRED RETURNS IN
# WIZARD IN TROUBLE!

# COMING SPRING 2020!